愿生如夏花

飞鸟集

STRAY BIRDS 中英对照版

〔印〕泰戈尔 ◎ 著　郑振铎 ◎ 译

石油工业出版社

图书在版编目（CIP）数据

愿生如夏花：飞鸟集 /（印）泰戈尔著；郑振铎译. — 北京：石油工业出版社，2020.1

ISBN 978-7-5183-3708-8

Ⅰ.①愿… Ⅱ.①泰…②郑… Ⅲ.①诗集-印度-现代 Ⅳ.① I351.25

中国版本图书馆 CIP 数据核字（2019）第 246056 号

责任编辑：	杨建君
制　　作：	（www.rzbook.com）
出版发行：	石油工业出版社
	（北京安定门外安华里 2 区 1 号楼　100011）
网　　址：	www.petropub.com
编辑部：	（010）64523616　64252031
图书营销中心：	（010）64523731　64523633
经　　销：	全国新华书店
印　　刷：	艺堂印刷（天津）有限公司

2020 年 1 月第 1 版　2020 年 1 月第 1 次印刷
880×1280 毫米　开本：1/32　印张：7
字数：150 千字
定价：49.00 元

版权所有，翻印必究

本书若出现印装质量问题，请与我社联系调换。
电话：（010）82021443

编者序

籁籁流年,转角悲欢。凝固在春夏秋冬里的文字,倾诉的是一代又一代人的生死喜怒,就像《飞鸟集》。

和被镌刻在泰戈尔冠冕上、煊赫雍容的《吉檀迦利》不同,创作于1913年、初版于1916年的《飞鸟集》,骨子里蕴藏的是一种洗尽铅华之后的沉静与从容。它诞生于泰戈尔人生最得意、也最失意的阶段,承载了太多的故事、历经了太多的悲欢流岚……

读《飞鸟集》,就像是在览阅一个世界。沙沙的笔端,既见清丽,也见奇崛;既有光明,也不乏黑暗。走在那用诗之芳尘铺就的道路上,无论康庄,抑或羊肠,屈曲盘折间,通向的都是同一处净土、同一簇烟火、同一片蓝天。那里,烙印着泰戈尔的至真、至纯。

"所有诗人,都是长不大的孩童",或许真的是这样吧。因为太过天真烂漫,泰戈尔才能把文字化作"天使的脸颜",掩藏了地狱的种种磨难,只绽放那如夏花般绚烂的笑靥。

与其说《飞鸟集》是一本正正经经的诗集,倒不如说它是泰戈尔多彩人生的见证。在这长短错落、凌乱而又统一的段段文字中,我们恍惚间便已照见那个出身名门、生性倔强、崇尚自由、文采斐然的身影。

他说:"我的心是旷野的鸟,在你的眼睛里找到了它的天空。"他说:"天空没有留下鸟的痕迹,但我已经飞过。"他用对生命的体验与感悟为自己,也为他人建造了一个从天堂垂向大地的鸟巢,这个巢,就是《飞鸟集》。书中的325首无题小诗,像是325棵巢草,纵横交杂、底色斑斓,又浑融如一。

这些诗,歌咏的都是极常见的物象:落叶、星辰、河流、云朵、飞鸟、浓雾、太阳、玫瑰、蟋蟀、瀑布、露珠,凡此种种,但他从这庸常中看到了新意,看到了哲理,看到了生死之间的妙谛。

虽然,命途的坎坷让泰戈尔心中常怀激愤,但他愿意用爱与宽容来化解。他对自己说"只有经历过地狱般的磨砺,才能练就天堂的力量;只有流过血的手指,才能弹出世间的绝响"。《飞鸟集》便是他为世人构架的"天堂"之一,其中不乏苦痛,却始终充满了自由、美好、和谐的基调。诗中的一草一木、一花一鸟都充斥着他的情感,是他诚挚的、真实的代言。

借由《飞鸟集》,我们与真实的泰戈尔不期而遇。不得不说,这是一种庆幸,而常怀此种庆幸之人,不论西东、不知凡几。

1922年,著名文学家、翻译家郑振铎先生将《飞鸟集》引入中国,从那之后，这本由部分《碎玉集》格言诗和英文短诗综合而成的诗集就在中国诗坛掀起了一股又一股的思想风暴，对郭沫若、徐志摩、冰心等现当代中国诗人的创作产生了深刻的影响。纵便是近百年后的今天，再次翻开那微微泛黄的纸笺，重读泰戈尔的这部经典，依旧仿佛漫步于一个壮阔而斑斓的世界，气象万千里见柔情，醍醐灌顶处见哲思，既感至真至简，又觉包罗万象，以至现今中外，无数人为之如痴如醉，也无怪其能被译成各种版本，行销全世界。

细细品读《飞鸟集》，其实不难发现，这本看似有些芜杂、凌乱、缺乏中心主题的格言诗集，字里行间却充斥着一种振奋人心、积极向上、温暖而蕴藉的力量。面对伤痛，它谆谆细嘱："让我设想，在群星之中，有一颗星星是指导着我的生命通过不可知的黑暗的。"对于爱情，它侃侃而言："不要因为峭壁是高的，而让你的爱情坐在峭壁上。"谈起人生，它悠然从容："群星不怕显得像萤火虫那样。"论起名利，它淡泊清冷："鸟翼系上黄金，这鸟儿便永远不能再在天上翱翔。"对于愁苦，它温言慰藉："纵然伤心，也不要愁眉不展，因为你不知是谁会爱上你的笑容。"凡此种种，不一而足。

或许，这种力量并不能感染所有的人，但它能让绝大部分人心向光明。

当然，"一千个人眼中即有一千个哈姆雷特"。有人觉得它是传世经典、光耀千秋，也有人觉得它就是富贵闲人的无病呻吟、华而不实；

有人觉得它是对世界、对人生、对自然与爱最真纯的探索，也有人觉得它就是泛神论者的不知所云、徒具虚名。万种千般看法，终归莫衷一是。

一书一世界，这个世界究竟是荒芜、是美丽、是辽远、是逼仄、是纯白、是黝黑、是温暖、是冷漠，别人说的都不算，唯有自己读过、品过、揣摩过、深思过才算。

所以，亲爱的你，若是有暇，不妨在某个阳光温醇的午后，备一杯香茗，静静地将本书翻开，看一看"从未拒绝生命，且能将生命说出"的泰戈尔用生命与阅历编织的"鸟巢"究竟是何模样，无论你最后是爱上、恨上还是恋上。

目录

辑一

飞鸟集　• 001

辑二

生如夏花之绚烂　• 209

辑一

飞鸟集
Stray Birds

1

夏天的飞鸟,

飞到我窗前唱歌,又飞走了。

秋天的黄叶,它们没有什么可唱,

只叹息一声,飞落在那里。

Stray birds of summer come to my window

to sing and fly away.

And yellow leaves of autumn,

which have no songs,

flutter and fall there with a sigh.

2

世界上的一队小小的漂泊者呀,
请留下你们的足印在我的文字里。

O troupe of little vagrants of the world,
leave your footprints in my words.

3

世界对着它的爱人,把它浩翰的面具揭下了。
它变小了,小如一首歌,小如一回永恒的接吻。

The world puts off its mask of vastness to its lover.
It becomes small as one song, as one kiss of the eternal.

4

是大地的泪点,
使她的微笑保持着青春不谢。

It is the tears of the earth that
keep her smiles in bloom.

5

无垠的沙漠热烈追求一叶绿草的爱,
她摇摇头笑着飞开了。

The mighty desert is burning for the love of a blade
of grass who shakes her head and laughs and flies away.

6

如果你因失去了太阳而流泪,
那么你也将失去群星了。

If you shed tears when you miss the sun,
you also miss the stars.

7

跳舞着的流水呀,在你途中的泥沙,要求你的歌声,你的流动呢。你肯挟跛足的泥沙而俱下吗?

The sands in your way beg for your song and your movement, dancing water. Will you carry the burden of their lameness?

8

她的热切的脸,如夜雨似的,
搅扰着我的梦魂。

Her wishful face haunts my dreams
like the rain at night.

9

有一次,我们梦见大家都是不相识的。
我们醒了,却知道我们原是相亲相爱的。

Once we dreamt that we were strangers.
We wake up to find that we were dear to each other.

10

忧思在我的心里平静下去,
正如暮色降临在寂静的山林中。

Sorrow is hushed into peace in my heart like the evening among the silent trees.

11

有些看不见的手指,如懒懒的微飔似的,
正在我的心上奏着潺湲的乐声。

Some unseen fingers, like an idle breeze, are playing upon my heart the music of the ripples.

12

"海水呀,你说的是什么?"

"是永恒的疑问。"

"天空呀,你回答的话是什么?"

"是永恒的沉默。"

"What language is thine, O sea?"

"The language of eternal question."

"What language is thy answer, O sky?"

"The language of eternal silence."

13

静静地听,我的心呀,听那世界的低语,
这是它对你求爱的表示呀。

Listen, my heart,

to the whispers of the world with which it makes love to you.

14

创造的神秘,有如夜间的黑暗——是伟大的。
而知识的幻影却不过如晨间之雾。

The mystery of creation is like the darkness of night—it is great. Delusions of knowledge are like the fog of the morning.

15

不要因为峭壁是高的,
便让你的爱情坐在峭壁上。

Do not seat your love upon a precipice
because it is high.

16

我今晨坐在窗前,世界如一个过路人似的,
停留了一会,向我点点头又走过去了。

I sit at my window this morning where the world like
a passer-by stops for a moment, nods to me and goes.

17

这些微思,是树叶的簌簌之声呀;
它们在我的心里欢悦地微语着。

These little thoughts are the rustle of leaves;
they have their whisper of joy in my mind.

18

你看不见你自己,
你所看见的只是你的影子。

What you are you do not see,
what you see is your shadow.

19

神呀,我的那些愿望真是愚傻呀,

它们杂在你的歌声中喧叫着呢。

让我只是静听着吧。

My wishes are fools,

they shout across the songs, my Master.

Let me but listen.

20

我不能选择那最好的。

是那最好的选择我。

I cannot choose the best.

The best chooses me.

21

那些把灯背在背上的人,
把他们的影子投到了自己前面。

They throw their shadows before them
who carry their lantern on their back.

22

我的存在,对我是一个永久的神奇,
这就是生活。

That I exist is a perpetual surprise which is life.

23

"我们萧萧的树叶都有声响回答那风和雨。
你是谁呢,那样地沉默着?"
"我不过是一朵花。"

"We, the rustling leaves,
have a voice that answers the storms,
but who are you so silent?"
"I am a mere flower."

24

休息与工作的关系,
正如眼睑与眼睛的关系。

Rest belongs to the work as
the eyelids to the eyes.

25

人是一个初生的孩子,
他的力量,就是生长的力量。

Man is a born child,
his power is the power of growth.

26

神希望我们酬答他,

在于他送给我们的花朵,而不在于太阳和土地。

God expects answers for the flowers he sends us,

not for the sun and the earth.

27

光明如一个裸体的孩子,

快快活活地在绿叶当中游戏,它不知道人是会欺诈的。

The light that plays, like a naked child,

among the green leaves happily knows not that man can lie.

28

啊,美呀,在爱中找你自己吧,
不要到你镜子的谄谀中去找寻。

O Beauty, find thyself in love,
not in the flattery of thy mirror.

29

我的心把她的波浪在世界的海岸上冲激着,
以热泪在上边写着她的题记:"我爱你。"

My heart beats her waves at the shore of the world and writes upon it her signature in tears with the words, "I love thee."

30

"月儿呀,你在等候什么呢?"
"向我将让位给他的太阳致敬。"

"Moon, for what do you wait?"
"To salute the sun for whom I must make way."

31

绿树长到了我的窗前,
仿佛是喑哑的大地发出的渴望的声音。

The trees come up to my window like
the yearning voice of the dumb earth.

32

神自己的清晨,在他自己看来也是新奇的。

His own mornings are new surprises to God.

33

生命从世界得到资产,
爱情使它得到价值。

Life finds its wealth by the claims of the world,
and its worth by the claims of love.

34

枯竭的河床,并不感谢它的过去。

The dry river-bed finds no thanks for its past.

35

鸟儿愿为一朵云。
云儿愿为一只鸟。

The bird wishes it were a cloud.
The cloud wishes it were a bird.

36

瀑布歌唱道:"我得到自由时便有歌声了。"

The waterfall sing,
"I find my song, when I find my freedom."

37

我说不出这心为什么那样默默地颓丧着。
是为了它那不曾要求,不曾知道、
不曾记得的小小的需要。

I cannot tell why this heart languishes in silence.
It is for small needs it never asks,
or knows or remembers.

38

妇人，你在料理家事的时候，你的手足歌唱着，

正如山间的溪水歌唱着在小石中流过。

Woman, when you move about in your household

service your limbs sing like a hill stream among its pebbles.

39

当太阳横过西方的海面时，

对着东方留下他的最后的敬礼。

The sun goes to cross the Western sea,

leaving its last salutation to the East.

40

不要因为你自己没有胃口而去责备你的食物。

Do not blame your food because you have no appetite.

41

群树如表示大地的愿望似的,
踮起脚来向天空窥望。

The trees, like the longings of the earth,
stand a tiptoe to peep at the heaven.

42

你微微地笑着,不同我说什么话。

而我觉得,

为了这个,我已等待得久了。

You smiled and talked to me of nothing and I felt that for this I had been waiting long.

43

水里的游鱼是沉默的,

陆地上的兽类是喧闹的,

空中的飞鸟是歌唱着的。

但是,人类却兼有海里的沉默、

地上的喧闹与空中的音乐。

The fish in the water is silent,

the animal on the earth is noisy,

the bird in the air is singing.

But Man has in him the silence of the sea,

the noise of the earth and the music of the air.

44

世界在踌躇之心的琴弦上跑过去，
奏出忧郁的乐声。

The world rushes on over the strings of the lingering heart making the music of sadness.

45

他把他的刀剑当作他的上帝。
当他的刀剑胜利时他自己却失败了。

He has made his weapons his gods.
When his weapons win he is defeated himself.

46

神从创造中找到他自己。

God finds himself by creating.

47

阴影戴上她的面幕,

秘密地,温顺地,

用她的沉默的爱的脚步,跟在"光"后面。

Shadow, with her veil drawn,

follows Light in secret meekness,

with her silent steps of love.

48

群星不怕显得像萤火那样。

The stars are not afraid to appear like fireflies.

49

谢谢神,我不是一个权力的轮子,
而是被压在这轮下的活人之一。

I thank thee that I am none of the wheels of power
but I am one with the living creatures
that are crushed by it.

50

心是尖锐的,不是宽博的,

它执着在每一点上,却并不活动。

The mind, sharp but not broad,

sticks at every point but does not move.

51

你的偶像委散在尘土中了,

这可证明神的尘土比你的偶像还伟大。

Your idol is shattered in the dust to prove

that God's dust is greater than your idol.

52

人不能在他的历史中表现出他自己，
他在历史中奋斗着露出头角。

Man does not reveal himself in his history,
he struggles up through it.

53

玻璃灯因为瓦灯叫它做表兄而责备瓦灯,
但当明月出来时,玻璃灯却温和地微笑着,
叫明月为——"我亲爱的,亲爱的姐姐。"

While the glass lamp rebukes the earthen
for calling it cousin, the moon rises,
and the glass lamp, with a bland smile,
calls her, — "My dear, dear sister."

54

我们如海鸥之与波涛相遇似的,遇见了,走近了。
海鸥飞去,波涛滚滚地流开,我们也分别了。

Like the meeting of the seagulls and the waves
we meet and come near. The seagulls fly off,
the waves roll away and we depart.

55

我的白昼已经完了,我像一只泊在海滩上的小船,
谛听着晚潮跳舞的乐声。

My day is done, and I am like a boat drawn on the beach,
listening to the dance-music of
the tide in the evening.

56

我们的生命是天赋的,

我们唯有献出生命,才能得到生命。

Life is given to us,

we earn it by giving it.

57

当我们是大为谦卑的时候,

便是我们最近于伟大的时候。

We come nearest to the great when

we are great in humility.

58

麻雀看见孔雀负担着它的翎尾，
替它担忧。

The sparrow is sorry for the peacock
at the burden of its tail.

59

决不要害怕刹那——永恒之声这样唱着。

Never be afraid of the moments —
thus sings the voice of the everlasting.

60

飓风于无路之中寻求最短之路,
又突然地在"无何有之国"终止了它的寻求。

The hurricane seeks the shortest road by the no-road,
and suddenly ends its search in the Nowhere.

61

在我自己的杯中,饮了我的酒吧,朋友。
一倒在别人的杯里,这酒的腾跳的泡沫便要消失了。

Take my wine in my own cup, friend.
It loses its wreath of foam when poured into that of others.

62

"完全"为了对"不全"的爱,
把自己装饰得美丽。

The perfect decks itself in beauty
for the love of the Imperfect.

63

神对人说道:"我医治你所以伤害你,
爱你所以惩罚你。"

God says to man, "I heal you therefore I hurt,
love you therefore punish."

64

谢谢火焰给你光明,但是不要忘了那执灯的人,
他是坚忍地站在黑暗当中呢。

Thank the flame for its light,
but do not forget the lampholder standing
in the shade with constancy of patience.

65

小草呀,你的足步虽小,
但是你拥有你足下的土地。

Tiny grass, your steps are small,
but you possess the earth under your tread.

66

幼花的蓓蕾开放了，它叫道：
"亲爱的世界呀，请不要萎谢了。"

The infant flower opens its bud and cries,
"Dear World, please do not fade."

67

神对于那些大帝国会感到厌恶，
却决不会厌恶那些小小的花朵。

God grows weary of great kingdoms,
but never of little flowers.

68

错误经不起失败,
但是真理却不怕失败。

Wrong cannot afford defeat but Right can.

69

瀑布歌唱道:"虽然渴者只要少许的水便够了,
我却很快活地给予了我全部的水。"

"I give my whole water in joy," sings the waterfall,
"though little of it is enough for the thirsty."

70

把那些花朵抛掷上去的那一阵子无休无止的狂欢大喜的劲儿,其源泉是在哪里呢?

Where is the fountain that throws up these flowers in a ceaseless outbreak of ecstasy?

71

樵夫的斧头,问树要斧柄。
树便给了它。

The woodcutter's axe begged for its handle from the tree.
The tree gave it.

72

这寂独的黄昏,幕着雾与雨,
我在我心的孤寂里,
感觉到它的叹息。

In my solitude of heart I feel the sigh of this widowed evening veiled with mist and rain.

73

贞操是从丰富的爱情中生出来的财富。

Chastity is a wealth that comes from abundance of love.

74

雾,像爱情一样,在山峰的心上游戏,
生出种种美丽的变幻。

The mist, like love, plays upon the heart
of the hills and bring out surprises of beanty.

75

我们把世界看错了,反说它欺骗我们。

We read the world wrong and say that it deceives us.

76

诗人——飙风,正出经海洋和森林,
追求它自己的歌声。

The poet wind is out over the sea and the forest
to seek his own voice.

77

每一个孩子出生时都带来信息说:
神对人并未灰心失望。

Every child comes with the message that God
is not yet discouraged of man.

78

绿草求她地上的伴侣。

树木求他天空的寂寞。

The grass seeks her crowd in the earth.

The tree seeks his solitude of the sky.

79

人对他自己建筑起堤防来。

Man barricades against himself.

80

我的朋友,你的语声飘荡在我的心里,
像那海水的低吟声绕缭在静听着的松林之间。

Your voice, my friend, wanders in my heart,
like the muffled sound of the sea among these listening pines.

81

这个不可见的黑暗之火焰,
以繁星为其火花的,到底是什么呢?

What is this unseen flame of darkness whose sparks are the stars?

82

使生如夏花之绚烂,死如秋叶之静美。

Let life be beautiful like summer flowers and death like autumn leaves.

83

那想做好人的,在门外敲着门;
那爱人的,看见门敞开着。

He who wants to do good knocks at the gate;
he who loves finds the gate open.

84

在死的时候,众多合而为一;
在生的时候,一化为众多。
神死了的时候,宗教便将合而为一。

In death the many becomes one;
in life the one becomes many.
Religion will be one when God is dead.

85

艺术家是自然的情人,
所以他是自然的奴隶,也是自然的主人。

The artist is the lover of Nature,
 therefore he is her slave and her master.

86

"你离我有多远呢,果实呀?"
"我藏在你心里呢,花呀。"

"How far are you from me, O Fruit?"
"I am hidden in your heart, O Flower."

87

这个渴望是为了那个在黑夜里感觉得到、
在大白天里却看不见的人。

This longing is for the one who is felt in the dark,
but not seen in the day.

88

露珠对湖水说道:"你是在荷叶下面的大露珠,
我是在荷叶上面较小的露珠。"

"You are the big drop of dew under the lotus leaf,
I am the smaller one on its upper side,"
said the dew drop to the lake.

89

刀鞘保护刀的锋利,
它自己则满足于它的迟钝。

The scabbard is content to be dull
when it protects the keenness of the sword.

90

在黑暗中,"一"视若一体;
在光亮中,"一"便视若众多。

In darkness the One appears as uniform;
in the light the One appears as manifold.

91

大地借助于绿草,
显出她自己的殷勤好客。

The great earth makes herself hospitable
with the help of the grass.

92

绿叶的生与死乃是旋风的急骤的旋转，
它的更广大的旋转的圈子乃是在天上繁星之间徐缓地转动。

The birth and death of the leaves are the rapid
whirls of the eddy whose wider circles
move slowly among stars.

93

权势对世界说道:"你是我的。"

世界便把权势囚禁在她的宝座下面。

爱情对世界说道:"我是你的。"

世界便给予爱情以在她屋内来往的自由。

Power said to the world, "You are mine."

The world kept it prisoner on her throne.

Love said to the world, "I am thine."

The world gave it the freedom of her house.

94

浓雾仿佛是大地的愿望。

它藏起了太阳,而太阳原是她所呼求的。

The mist is like the earth's desire.

It hides the sun for whom she cries.

95

安静些吧,我的心,

这些大树都是祈祷者呀。

Be still, my heart,

these great trees are prayers.

96

瞬刻的喧声,讥笑着永恒的音乐。

The noise of the moment scoffs at the music
of the Eternal.

97

我想起了浮泛在生与爱与死的川流上的许多别的时代,以及这些时代之被遗忘,我便感觉到离开尘世的自由了。

I think of other ages that floated upon the stream of life
and love and death and are forgotten, and I feel
the freedom of passing away.

98

我灵魂里的忧郁就是她的新婚的面纱。

这面纱等候着在夜间卸去。

The sadness of my soul is her bride's veil.

It waits to be lifted in the night.

99

死之印记给生的钱币以价值,

使它能够用生命来购买那真正的宝物。

Death's stamp gives value to the coin of life,

making it possible to buy with life what is truly precious.

100

白云谦逊地站在天之一隅。

晨光给它戴上了霞彩。

The cloud stood humbly in a corner of the sky.

The morning crowned it with splendour.

101

尘土受到损辱,却以她的花朵来报答。

The dust receives insult and in return offers her flowers.

102

只管走过去,不必逗留着去采了花朵来保存,
因为一路上,花朵自会继续开放的。

Do not linger to gather flowers to keep them,
but walk on, for flowers will keep themselves blooming
all your way.

103

根是地下的枝。
枝是空中的根。

Roots are the branches down in the earth.
Branches are roots in the air.

104

远远去了的夏之音乐,

翱翔于秋间,寻求它的旧垒。

The music of the far-away summer flutters around the autumn seeking its former nest.

105

不要从你自己的袋里掏出勋绩借给你的朋友,

这是污辱他的。

Do not insult your friend by lending him merits from your own pocket.

106

无名日子的感触,攀缘在我的心上,
正像那绿色的苔藓,攀缘在老树的周身。

The touch of the nameless days clings to my heart
like mosses round the old tree.

107

回声嘲笑她的原声,以证明她是原声。

The echo mocks her origin to prove
she is the original.

108

当富贵利达的人夸说他得到神的特别恩惠时,
上帝却羞了。

God is ashamed when the prosperous boasts
of his special favour.

109

我投射我自己的影子在我的路上,
因为我有一盏还没有燃点起来的明灯。

I cast my own shadow upon my path,
because I have a lamp that has not been lighted.

110

人走进喧哗的群众里去,
为的是要淹没他自己的沉默的呼号。

Man goes into the noisy crowed to drown
his own clamor of silence.

111

终止于衰竭是"死亡",
但"圆满"却终止于无穷。

That which ends in exhaustion is death,
but the perfect ending is in the endless.

112

太阳只穿一件朴素的光衣,

白云却披了灿烂的裙裾。

The sun has his simple rode of light.

The clouds are decked with gorgeousness.

113

山峰如群儿之喧嚷,举起他们的双臂,

想去捉天上的星星。

The hills are like shouts of children

who raise their arms, trying to catch stars.

114

道路虽然拥挤,却是寂寞的,
因为它是不被爱的。

The road is lonely in its crowd for it is not loved.

115

权势以它的恶行自夸,
落下的黄叶与浮游的云片却在笑它。

The power that boasts of its mischiefs is laughed
at by the yellow leaves that fall, and clouds that pass by.

116

今天大地在太阳光里向我营营哼鸣,

像一个织着布的妇人,

用一种已经被忘却的语言,

哼着一些古代的歌曲。

The earth hums to me today in the sun,

like a woman at her spinning,

some ballad of the ancient time in a forgotten tongue.

117

绿草是无愧于它所生长的伟大世界的。

The grass-blade is worthy of the great world where it grows.

118

梦是一个一定要谈话的妻子。
睡眠是一个默默忍受的丈夫。

Dream is a wife who must talk.
Sleep is a husband who silently suffers.

119

夜与逝去的日子接吻,

轻轻地在他耳旁说道:"我是死,

是你的母亲。我就要给你以新的生命。"

The night kisses the fading day whispering to his ear,

"I am death, your mother.

I am to give you fresh birth."

120

黑夜呀,我感觉到你的美了。你的美如一个可爱的妇人,

当她把灯灭了的时候。

I feel thy beauty, dark night,

like that of the loved woman when she has put out the lamp.

121

我把在那些已逝去的世界上的繁荣带到我的世界上来。

I carry in my world that flourishes the worlds
that have failed.

122

亲爱的朋友呀，当我静听着海涛时，
我好几次在暮色深沉的黄昏里，
在这个海岸上，感到你的伟大思想的沉默了。

Dear friend, I feel the silence of your great thoughts
of many a deepening eventide on this beach
when I listen to these waves.

123

鸟以为把鱼举在空中是一种慈善的举动。

The bird thinks it is an act of kindness to give the fish a life in the air.

124

夜对太阳说道:"在月亮中,你送了你的情书给我。"
"我已在绿草上留下我的流着泪点的回答了。"

"In the moon thou sendest thy love letters to me," said the night to the sun.
"I leave my answers in tears upon the grass."

125

伟人是一个天生的孩子，
当他死时，他把他的伟大的孩提时代给了世界。

The great is a born child; when he dies
he gives his great childhood to the world.

126

不是槌的打击，乃是水的载歌载舞，
使鹅卵石臻于完美。

Not hammer-strokes,
but dance of the water sings the pebbles into perfection.

127

蜜蜂从花中啜蜜,离开时嘤嘤地道谢。

浮华的蝴蝶却相信花是应该向它道谢的。

Bees sip honey from flowers and hum their thanks when they leave.

The gaudy butterfly is sure that the flowers owe thanks to him.

128

如果你不等待着要说出完全的真理,

那么把真话说出来是很容易的。

To be outspoken is easy when you do not wait to speak the complete truth.

129

"可能"问"不可能"道:"你住在什么地方呢?"
它回答道:"在那无能为力者的梦境里。"

Asks the Possible to the Impossible, "Where is your dwelling-place?"
"In the dreams of the impotent," comes the answer.

130

如果你把所有的错误都关在门外时,
真理也要被关在门外面了。

If you shut your door to all errors truth will be shut out.

131

我听见有些东西在我心的忧闷后面萧萧作响,
——我不能看见它们。

I hear some rustle of things behind my sadness of heart,
—I cannot see them.

132

闲暇在动作时便是工作。
静止的海水荡动时便成波涛。

Leisure in its activity is work.
The stillness of the sea stirs in waves.

133

绿叶恋爱时便成了花。

花崇拜时便成了果实。

The leaf becomes flower when it loves.

The flower becomes fruit when it worships.

134

埋在地下的树根使树枝产生果实,

却不要求什么报酬。

The roots below the earth claim no rewards

for making the branches fruitful.

135

阴雨的黄昏,风不休止地吹着。
我看着摇曳的树枝,感念着万物的伟大。

This rainy evening the wind is restless.
I look at the swaying branches and ponder over the greatness of all things.

136

子夜的风雨,如一个巨大的孩子,
在不合时宜的黑夜里醒来,开始游戏和喧闹。

Storm of midnight, like a giant child awakened in the untimely dark, has begun to play and shout.

137

海呀，你这暴风雨的孤寂的新妇呀，

你虽掀起波浪追随你的情人，但是无用呀。

Thou raisest thy waves vainly to follow thy lover,

O sea, thou lonely bride of the storm.

138

文字对工作说道:"我惭愧我的空虚。"
工作对文字说道:"当我看见你时,
我便知道我是怎样的贫乏了。"

"I am ashamed of my emptiness,"
said the Word to the Work.
"I know how poor I am when I see you, "
said the Work to the Word.

139

时间是变化的财富，时钟模仿它，
却只有变化而无财富。

Time is the wealth of change, but the clock
in its parody makes it mere change and no wealth.

140

真理穿了衣裳，觉得事实太拘束了。
在想象中，她却转动得很舒畅。

Truth in her dress finds facts too tight.
In fiction she moves with ease.

141

当我到这里那里旅行着时,
路呀,我厌倦你了;
但是现在,当你引导我到各处去时,
我便爱上你,与你结婚了。

When I travelled to here and to there,
I was tired of thee, O Road,but now
when thou leadest me to everywhere I am
wedded to thee in love.

142

让我设想,在群星之中,
有一颗星是指导着我的生命通过不可知的黑暗的。

Let me think that there is one among those stars that guides my life through the dark unknown.

143

妇人,你用了你美丽的手指,触着我的什物,
秩序便如音乐似的生出来了。

Woman, with the grace of your fingers you touched my things and order came out like music.

144

一个忧郁的声音,筑巢于逝水似的年华中。

它在夜里向我唱道:"我爱你。"

One sad voice has its nest among the ruins of the years.

It sings to me in the night,

—— "I loved you."

145

燃着的火,以它熊熊的光焰警告我不要走近它。

把我从潜藏在灰中的余烬里救出来吧。

The flaming fire warns me off by its own glow.

Save me from the dying embers hidden under ashes.

146

我有群星在天上。

但是,唉,我屋里的小灯却没有点亮。

I have my stars in the sky.

But oh for my little lamp unlit in my house.

147

死文字的尘土沾着你。

用沉默去洗净你的灵魂吧。

The dust of the dead words clings to thee.

Wash thy soul with silence.

148

生命里留了许多罅隙,

从中送来了死之忧郁的音乐。

Gaps are left in life through which

comes the sad music of death.

149

世界已在早晨敞开了它的光明之心。

出来吧,我的心,带着你的爱去与它相会。

The world has opened its heart of light in the morning.

Come out, my heart, with thy love to meet it.

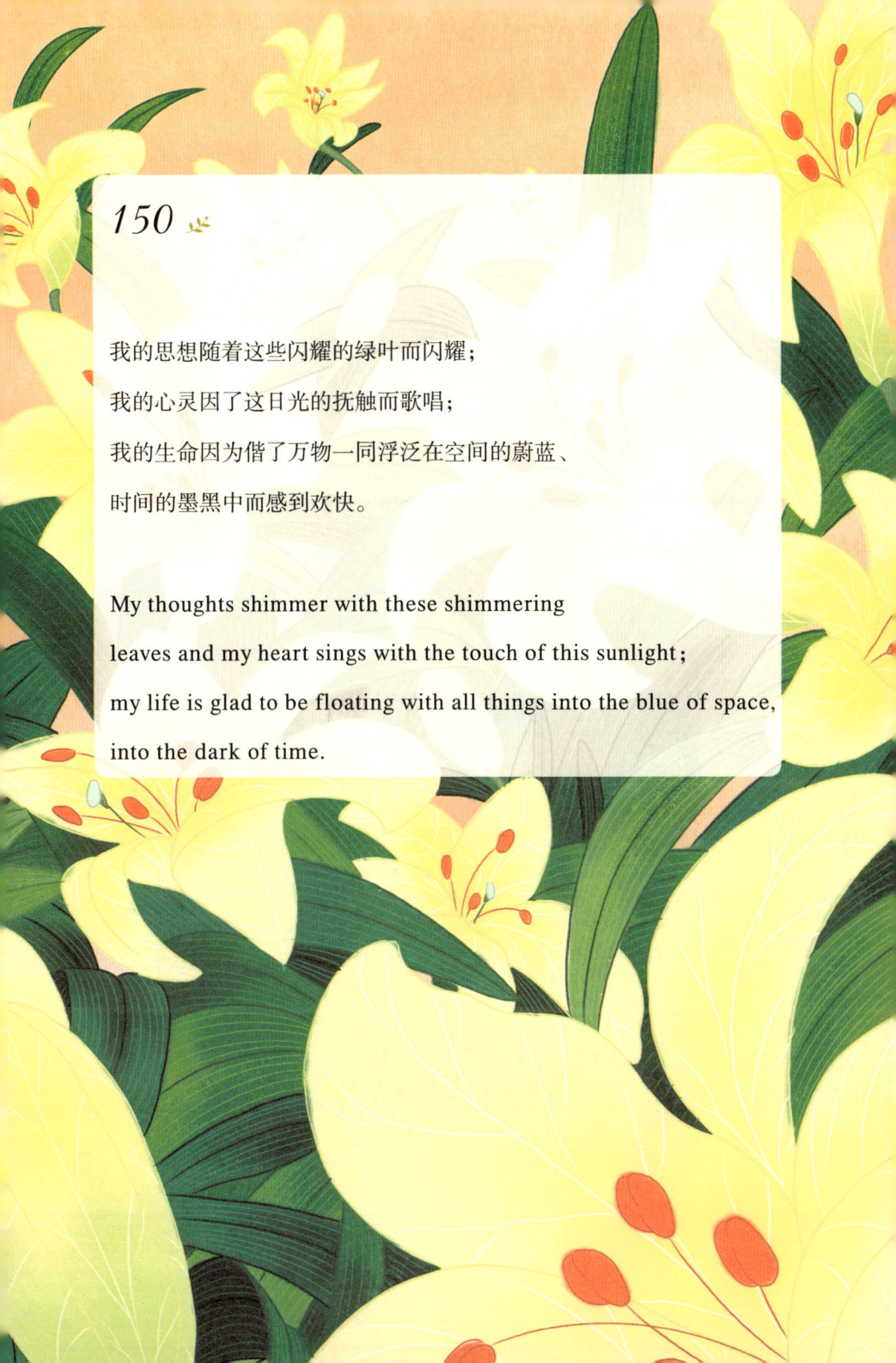

150

我的思想随着这些闪耀的绿叶而闪耀；

我的心灵因了这日光的抚触而歌唱；

我的生命因为借了万物一同浮泛在空间的蔚蓝、

时间的墨黑中而感到欢快。

My thoughts shimmer with these shimmering

leaves and my heart sings with the touch of this sunlight;

my life is glad to be floating with all things into the blue of space,

into the dark of time.

151

神的巨大的威权是在柔和的微飔里，
而不在狂风暴雨之中。

God's great power is in the gentle breeze,
not in the storm.

152

在梦中,一切事都散漫着,

都压着我,但这不过是一个梦呀。

当我醒来时,我便将觉得这些事都已聚集在你那里,

我也便将自由了。

This is a dream in which things are all loose and they oppress.

I shall find them gathered in thee when

I awake and shall be free.

153

落日问道：

"有谁继续我的职务呢？"

瓦灯说道：

"我要尽我所能地做去，我的主人。"

"Who is there to take up my duties?"
asked the setting sun.
"I shall do what I can, my Master,"
said the earthen lamp.

154

采着花瓣时，得不到花的美丽。

By plucking her petals you do not gather the beauty of the flower.

155

沉默蕴蓄着语声，
正如鸟巢拥围着睡鸟。

Silence will carry your voice like the nest that holds the sleeping birds.

156

大的不怕与小的同游。

居中的却远而避之。

The Great walks with the Small without fear.

The Middling keeps aloof.

157

夜秘密地把花开放了,

却让那白日去领受谢词。

The night opens the flowers in secret

and allows the day to get thanks.

158

权势认为牺牲者的痛苦是忘恩负义。

Power takes as ingratitude the writhings
of its victims.

159

当我们以我们的充实为乐时,
那么,我们便能很快乐地跟我们的果实分手了。

When we rejoice in our fullness,
then we can part with our fruits with joy.

160

雨点吻着大地,微语道:
"我们是你的思家的孩子,母亲,
现在从天上回到你这里来了。"

The raindrops kissed the earth and whispered,
—"We are thy homesick children, mother,
come back to thee from the heaven."

161

蛛网好像要捉露点,
却捉住了苍蝇。

The cobweb pretends to catch
dewdrops and catches flies.

162

爱情呀！当你手里拿着点亮了的痛苦之灯走来时，我能够看见你的脸，而且以你为幸福。

Love! When you come with the burning lamp of pain in your hand, I can see your face and know you as bliss.

163

萤火对天上的星说道：
"学者说你的光明总有一天会消灭的。"
天上的星不回答它。

"The leaned say that your lights will one day be no more,"
said the firefly to the stars.
The stars made no answer.

164

在黄昏的微光里，
有那清晨的鸟儿来到了我的沉默的鸟巢里。

In the dusk of the evening the bird of some
early dawn comes to the nest of my silence.

165

思想掠过我的心上,如一群野鸭飞过天空。
我听见它们鼓翼之声了。

Thoughts pass in my mind like flocks of ducks in the sky.
I hear the voice of their wings.

166

沟洫总喜欢想:
河流的存在,是专为它供给水流的。

The canal loves to think that
rivers exist solely to supply it with water.

167

世界以它的痛苦同我接吻,
而要求歌声做报酬。

The world has kissed my soul with its pain,
asking for its return in songs.

168

压迫着我的,到底是我的想要外出的灵魂呢,
还是那世界的灵魂,敲着我心的门,想要进来呢?

That which oppresses me,
is it my soul trying to come out in the open,
or the soul of the world knocking at my heart for its entrance?

169

思想以它自己的言语喂养它自己而成长起来。

Thought feeds itself with its own
words and grows.

170

我把我的心之碗轻轻浸入这沉默之时刻中,
它盛满了爱了。

I have dipped the vessel of my heart into this silent hour;
it has filled with love.

171

或者你在工作,或者你没有。

当你不得不说"让我们做些事吧"时,那么就要开始胡闹了。

Either you have work or you have not.

When you have to say, "Let us do something,"

then begins mischief.

172

向日葵羞于把无名的花朵看作它的同胞。

太阳升上来了,向它微笑,说道:"你好吗,我的宝贝儿?"

The sunflower blushed to own the nameless flower as her kin.

The sun rose and smiled on it, saying,

"Are you well, my darling?"

173

"谁如命运似的催着我向前走呢？"
"那是我自己，在身背后大跨步走着。"

"Who drives me forward like fate?"
"The Myself striding on my back."

174

云把水倒在河的水杯里，
它们自己却藏在远山之中。

The clouds fill the water-cups of the river,
hiding themselves in the distant hills.

175

我一路走去,从我的水瓶中漏出水来。
只剩下极少极少的水供我回家使用了。

I spill water from my water jar as I walk on my way,
Very little remains for my home.

176

杯中的水是光辉的；

海中的水却是黑色的。

小理可以用文字来说清楚；

大理却只有沉默。

The water in a vessel is sparkling;

the water in the sea is dark.

The small truth has words that are clear;

the great truth has great silence.

177

你的微笑是你自己田园里的花,
你的谈吐是你自己山上的松林的萧萧;
但是你的心呀,却是那个女人,
那个我们全都认识的女人。

Your smile was the flowers of your own fields,
your talk was the rustle of your own mountain pines,
but your heart was the woman that we all know.

178

我把小小的礼物留给我所爱的人,
——大的礼物却留给一切的人。

It is the little things that I leave behind for my loved ones,
—great things are for everyone.

179

妇人呀,你用泪海包绕着世界的心,
正如大海包绕着大地。

Woman, thou hast encircled the world's heart
with the depth of thy tears as the sea has the earth.

180

太阳以微笑向我问候。

雨,它的忧闷的姐姐,向我的心谈话。

The sunshine greets me with a smile.

The rain, his sad sister, talks to my heart.

181

我的昼间之花,落下它那被遗忘的花瓣。

在黄昏中,这花成熟为一颗记忆的金果。

My flower of the day dropped its petals forgotten.

In the evening it ripens into a golden fruit of memory.

182

我像那夜间之路,

正静悄悄地谛听着记忆的足音。

I am like the road in the night listening to the footfalls of its memories in silence.

183

黄昏的天空,在我看来,像一扇窗户,一盏灯火,灯火背后的一次等待。

The evening sky to me is like a window, and a lighted lamp, and a waiting behind it.

184

太急于做好事的人,
反而找不到时间去做好人。

He who is too busy doing good
finds no time to be good.

185

我是秋云,空空地不载着雨水,
但在成熟的稻田中,可以看见我的充实。

I am the autumn cloud, empty of rain,
see my fulness in the field of ripened rice.

186

他们嫉妒,他们残杀,人反而称赞他们。

然而上帝却害了羞,

匆匆地把他的记忆埋藏在绿草下面。

They hated and killed and men praised them.
But God in shame hastens to hide its memory
under the green grass.

187

脚趾乃是舍弃了其过去的手指。

Toes are the fingers that have forsaken their past.

188

黑暗向光明旅行，
但是盲者却向死亡旅行。

Darkness travels towards light,
but blindness towards death.

189

小狗疑心大宇宙阴谋篡夺它的位置。

The pet dog suspects the universe for
scheming to take its place.

190

静静地坐着吧,我的心,不要扬起你的尘土。

让世界自己寻路向你走来。

Sit still, my heart, do not raise your dust.

Let the world find its way to you.

191

弓在箭要射出之前,低声对箭说道:

"你的自由就是我的自由。"

The bow whispers to the arrow before it speeds forth

— "Your freedom is mine."

192

妇人,在你的笑声里有着生命之泉的音乐。

Woman, in your laughter you have the music of the fountain of life.

193

全是理智的心,恰如一柄全是锋刃的刀。
它叫使用它的人手上流血。

A mind all logic is like a knife all blade.
It makes the hand bleed that uses it.

194

神爱人间的灯光甚于他自己的大星。

God loves man's lamp lights better than his own great stars.

195

这世界乃是为美之音乐所驯服了的、狂风骤雨的世界。

This world is the world of wild storms kept tame with the music of beauty.

196

晚霞向太阳说道:"我的心经了你的接吻,
便似金的宝箱了。"

"My heart is like the golden casket of thy kiss."
said the sunset cloud to the sun.

197

接触着,你许会杀害;
远离着,你许会占有。

By touching you may kill,
by keeping away you may possess.

198

蟋蟀的唧唧，夜雨的淅沥，

从黑暗中传到我的耳边，

好似我已逝的少年时代，

沙沙地来到我梦境中。

The cricket's chirp and the patter of rain

come to me through the dark,

like the rustle of dreams

from my past youth.

199

花朵向星辰落尽了的曙天叫道:
"我的露点全失落了。"

"I have lost my dewdrop,"
cries the flower to the morning sky
that has lost all its stars.

200

燃烧着的木块,熊熊地生出火光,
叫道:"这是我的花朵,我的死亡。"

The burning log bursts in flame and cries,
——"This is my flower, my death."

201

黄蜂认为邻蜂储蜜之巢太小。
他的邻人要他去建筑一个更小的。

The wasp thinks that
the honey-hive of the neighbouring bees is too small.
His neighbours ask him to build one still smaller.

202

河岸向河流说道:"我不能留住你的波浪,
让我保存你的足印在我心里吧。"

"I cannot keep your waves,"
says the bank to the river.
"Let me keep your footprints in my heart."

203

白日以这小小地球的喧扰,
淹没了整个宇宙的沉默。

The day, with the noise of this little earth,
drowns the silence of all worlds.

204

歌声在空中感到无限,

图画在地上感到无限,

诗呢,无论在空中、在地上都是如此。

因为诗的词句含有能走动的意义与能飞翔的音乐。

The song feels the infinite in the air,

the picture in the earth,

the poem in the air and the earth;

For its words have meaning that walks and music that soars.

205

太阳在西方落下时,
他的早晨的东方已静悄悄地站在他面前。

When the sun goes down to the West,
the East of his morning stands before him in silence.

206

让我不要错误地把自己放在我的世界里,
而使它反对我。

Let me not put myself wrongly to my world
and set it against me.

207

荣誉使我感到惭愧,
因为我暗地里求着它。

Praise shames me,
for I secretly beg for it.

208

当我没有什么事做时,便让我不做什么事,
不受骚扰地沉入安静深处吧,一如那海水沉默时海边的暮色。

Let my doing nothing when I have nothing to do
become untroubled in its depth of peace like the evening
in the seashore when the water is silent.

209

少女呀,你的淳朴,
如湖水之碧,表现出你的真理之深邃。

Maiden, your simplicity, like the blueness of the lake,
reveals your depth of truth.

210

最好的东西不是独来的。
它伴了所有的东西同来。

The best does not come alone.
It comes with the company of the all.

211

上帝的右手是慈爱的,
但是他的左手却可怕。

God's right hand is gentle,
but terrible is his left hand.

212

我的晚色从陌生的树木中走来,
它用我的晓星所不懂得的语言说话。

My evening came among the alien trees and spoke
in a language which my morning stars did not know.

213

夜之黑暗是一只口袋，
迸出黎明的金光。

Night's darkness is a bag that bursts with
the gold of the dawn.

214

我们的欲望把彩虹的颜色
借给那只不过是云雾的人生。

Our desire lends the colours of the rainbow
to the mere mists and vapours of life.

215

神等待着，要从人的手上
把他自己的花朵作为礼物赢得回去。

God waits to win back his own flowers
as gifts from man's hands.

216

我的忧思缠绕着我，
要问我它们自己的名字。

My sad thoughts tease me
asking me their own names.

217

果实的事业是尊贵的，
花的事业是甜美的；
但是让我做叶的事业吧，
叶是谦逊地、专心地垂着绿荫的。

The service of the fruit is precious,
the service of the flower is sweet,
but let my service be the service of the leaves
in its shade of humble devotion.

218

我的心向着阑珊的风张了帆,
要到无论何处的阴凉之岛去。

My heart has spread its sails to the idle winds
for the shadowy island of Anywhere.

219

独夫们是凶暴的,但人民是善良的。

Men are cruel, but Man is kind.

220

把我当作你的杯吧,

让我为了你,而且为了你的人而盛满水吧。

Make me thy cup and let my fulness
be for thee and for thine.

221

狂风暴雨像是在痛苦中的某个天神的哭声,
因为他的爱情被大地所拒绝。

The storm is like the cry of some god in pain
whose love the earth refuses.

222

世界不会流失,
因为死亡并不是一个罅隙。

The world does not leak
because death is not a crack.

223

生命因为付出了的爱情而更为富足。

Life has become richer by the love
that has been lost.

224

我的朋友,你伟大的心闪射出东方朝阳的光芒,
正如黎明中的一个积雪的孤峰。

My friend, your great heart shone with the sunrise of the East
like the snowy summit of a lonely hill in the dawn.

225

死之流泉,使生的止水跳跃。

The fountain of death

makes the still water of life play.

226

那些有一切东西而没有您的人,我的上帝,

在讥笑着那些没有别的东西而只有您的人呢。

Those who have everything but thee, my God,

laugh at those who have nothing but thyself.

227

生命的运动在它自己的音乐里得到它的休息。

The movement of life has its rest in its own music.

228

踢足只能从地上扬起尘土而不能得到收获。

Kicks only raise dust and not crops from the earth.

229

我们的名字,便是夜里海波上发出的光,
痕迹也不留就泯灭了。

Our names are the light that glows on the sea
waves at night and then dies without leaving its signature.

230

让睁眼看着玫瑰花的人也看看它的刺。

Let him only see the thorns
who has eyes to see the rose.

231

鸟翼上系上了黄金,

这鸟便永不能再在天上翱翔了。

Set the bird's wings with gold and it
will never again soar in the sky.

232

我们地方的荷花又在这陌生的水上开了花,
放出同样的清香,只是名字换了。

The same lotus of our clime blooms here in the alien water
with the same sweetness, under another name.

233

在心的远景里,那相隔的距离显得更广阔了。

In heart's perspective the distance looms large.

234

月儿把她的光明遍照在天上,
却留着她的黑斑给她自己。

The moon has her light all over the sky,
her dark spots to herself.

235

不要说"这是早晨",

就用一个"昨天"的名词把它打发掉。

你第一次看到它,

把它当作还没有名字的新生孩子吧。

Do not say, "It is morning,"

and dismiss it with a name of yesterday.

See it for the first time as a new-born child

that has no name.

236

青烟对天空夸口，灰烬对大地夸口，
都以为它们是火的兄弟。

Smoke boasts to the sky,

and Ashes to the earth,

that they are brothers to the fire.

237

雨点向茉莉花微语道："把我永久地留在你的心里吧。"
茉莉花叹息了一声，落在地上了。

The raindrop whispered to the jasmine,

"Keep me in your heart for ever."The jasmine sighed,

"Alas,"and dropped to the ground.

238

惬怯的思想呀,不要怕我。

我是一个诗人。

Timid thoughts, do not be afraid of me.

I am a poet.

239

我的心在朦胧的沉默里,

似乎充满了蟋蟀的鸣声——声音的灰暗的暮色。

The dim silence of my mind seems filled

with crickets'chirp— the grey twilight of sound.

240

爆竹呀，你对群星的侮蔑，

又跟着你自己回到地上来了。

Rockets, your insult to the stars follows

yourself back to the earth.

241

您曾经带领着我,穿过我白天的拥挤不堪的旅程,
而到达了我的黄昏的孤寂之境。
在通宵的寂静里,我等待着它的意义。

Thou hast led me through my crowded travels
of the day to my evening's loneliness.
I wait for its meaning through
the stillness of the night.

242

我们的生命就似渡过一个大海,

我们都相聚在这个狭小的舟中。

死时,我们便到了岸,各往各的世界去了。

This life is the crossing of a sea,

where we meet in the same narrow ship.

In death we reach the shore and go to our different worlds.

243

真理之川从它的错误之沟渠中流过。

The stream of truth flows through its channels

of mistakes.

244

今天我的心是在想家了,
在想着那跨过时间之海的那一个甜蜜的时候。

My heart is homesick today for the one sweet hour across the sea of time.

245

鸟的歌声是曙光从大地反响过去的回声。

The bird-song is the echo of the morning light back from the earth.

246

晨光问毛茛道：

"你是骄傲得不肯和我接吻吗？"

"Are you too proud to kiss me?"
the morning light asks the buttercup.

247

小花问道：

"我要怎样地对你唱，怎样地崇拜你呢，太阳呀？"
太阳答道："只要用你的纯洁的素朴的沉默。"

"How may I sing to thee and worship, O Sun?"
asked the little flower.
"By the simple silence of thy purity, " answered the sun.

248

当人是兽时,他比兽还坏。

Man is worse than an animal when he is an animal.

249

黑云受光的接吻时便变成天上的花朵。

Dark clouds become heaven's flowers
when kissed by light.

250

不要让刀锋讥笑它柄子的拙钝。

Let not the sword-blade mock its handle
for being blunt.

251

夜的沉默,如一个深深的灯盏,
银河便是它燃着的灯光。

The night's silence, like a deep lamp,
is burning with the light of its milky way.

252

死像大海的无限的歌声,

日夜冲击着生命光明岛的四周。

Around the sunny island of Life swells day and night

death's limitless song of the sea.

253

花瓣似的山峰在饮着日光,

这山岂不像一朵花吗?

Is not this mountain like a flower,

with its petals of hill, drinking the sunlight?

254

"真实"的含义被误解,轻重被倒置,那就成了"不真实"。

The real with its meaning read wrong
and emphasis misplaced is the unreal.

255

我的心呀,从世界的流动中找你的美吧,
正如那小船得到风与水的优美似的。

Find your beauty, my heart,
from the world's movement,
like the boat that has the grace of the wind and the water.

256

眼不以能视来骄人,
却以它们的眼镜来骄人。

The eyes are not proud of their sight
but of their eyeglasses.

257

我住在我的这个小小的世界里,
生怕使它再缩小一丁点儿。
把我抬举到您的世界里去吧,
让我有高高兴兴地失去我的一切的自由。

I live in this little world of mine
and am afraid to make it the least less.
Life me into thy world and let me have
the freedom gladly to lose my all.

258

虚伪永远不能凭借它生长在权力中而变成真实。

The false can never grow into truth
by growing in power.

259

我的心，同着它的歌的拍拍舐岸的波浪，
渴望着要抚爱这个阳光熙和的绿色世界。

My heart, with its lapping waves of song,
longs to caress this green world of the sunny day.

260

道旁的草，爱那天上的星吧，
你的梦境便可在花朵里实现了。

Wayside grass, love the star,
then your dreams will come out in flowers.

261

让你的音乐如一柄利刃，
直刺入市井喧扰的心中吧。

Let your music, like a sword, pierce the noise
of the market to its heart.

262

这树的颤动之叶,

触动着我的心,像一个婴儿的手指。

The trembling leaves of this tree touch my heart

like the fingers of an infant child.

263

小花睡在尘土里。

它寻求蛱蝶走的道路。

The little flower lies in the dust.

It sought the path of the butterfly.

264

我是在道路纵横的世界上。

夜来了。打开您的门吧,家之世界啊!

I am in the world of the roads.

The night comes. Open thy gate,

thou world of the home.

265

我已经唱过了您的白天的歌。

在黄昏时候,让我拿着您的灯走过风雨飘摇的道路吧。

I have sung the songs of thy day.

In the evening

let me carry thy lamp through the stormy path.

266

我不要求你进我的屋里。

你到我无量的孤寂里来吧,我的爱人!

I do not ask thee into the house.

Come into my infinite loneliness, my Lover.

267

死亡隶属于生命,正与生一样。

举足是走路,正如落足也是走路。

Death belongs to life as birth does.

The walk is in the raising of the foot as in the laying of it down.

268

我已经学会了你在花与阳光里微语的意义。
——再教我明白你在苦与死中所说的话吧。

I have learnt the simple meaning of thy whispers in flowers
and sunshine—teach me to know
thy words in pain and death.

269

夜的花朵来晚了,当早晨吻着她时,
她战栗着,叹息了一声,萎落在地上了。

The night's flower was late when the morning kissed her,
she shivered and sighed and dropped to the ground.

270

从万物的愁苦中,

我听见了"永恒母亲"的呻吟。

Through the sadness of all things

I hear the crooning of the Eternal Mother.

271

大地呀,我到你岸上时是一个陌生人,

住在你屋内时是一个宾客,离开你的门时是一个朋友。

I came to your shore as a stranger,

I lived in your house as a guest,

I leave your door as a friend, my earth.

272

当我去时,让我的思想到你那里来,
如那夕阳的余光,
映在沉默的星天的边上。

Let my thoughts come to you,
when I am gone, like the afterglow of sunset
at the margin of starry silence.

273

在我的心头燃点起那休憩的黄昏星吧,
然后让黑夜向我微语着爱情。

Light in my heart the evening star of rest and then let
the night whisper to me of love.

274

我是一个在黑暗中的孩子。

我从夜的被单里向您伸出我的双手,母亲。

I am a child in the dark.

I stretch my hands through the coverlet of night for thee, Mother.

275

白天的工作完了。

把我的脸掩藏在您的臂间吧,母亲。

让我入梦吧。

The day of work is done.

Hide my face in your arms, Mother. Let me dream.

276

集会时的灯光，点了很久，

会散时，灯便立刻灭了。

The lamp of meeting burns long;

it goes out in a moment at the parting.

277

当我死时，世界呀，请在你的沉默中，

替我留着"我已经爱过了"这句话吧。

One word keep for me in thy silence, O World,

when I am dead, "I have loved."

278

我们在热爱世界时便生活在这世界上。

We live in this world when we love it.

279

让死者有那不朽的名,
但让生者有那不朽的爱。

Let the dead have the immortality of fame,
but the living the immortality of love.

280

我看见你,像那半醒的婴孩在黎明的微光里看见他的母亲,于是微笑而又睡去了。

I have seen thee as the half-awakened child sees his mother in the dusk of the dawn and then smiles and sleeps again.

281

我将死了又死,以明白生是无穷无尽的。

I shall die again and again to know that life is inexhaustible.

282

当我和拥挤的人群一同在路上走过时,
我看见您从阳台上送过来的微笑。
我歌唱着,忘却了所有的喧哗。

While I was passing with the crowd in the road
I saw thy smile from the balcony and I sang
and forgot all noise.

283

爱就是充实了的生命,正如盛满了酒的酒杯。

Love is life in its fulness like the cup with its wine.

284

他们点了他们自己的灯,在他们的寺院内,

吟唱他们自己的话语。

但是小鸟们却在你的晨光中,

唱着你的名字——因为你的名字便是快乐。

They light their own lamps and sing their

own words in their temples.

But the birds sing thy name in thine own morning light,

—for thy name is joy.

285

领我到您的沉寂的中心,
使我的心充满了歌吧。

Lead me in the centre of thy silence to fill
my heart with songs.

286

让那些选择了他们自己的焰火咝咝的世界的,
就生活在那里吧。
我的心渴望着您的繁星,我的上帝。

Let them live who choose in their own hissing world
of fireworks.
My heart longs for thy stars, my God.

287

爱的痛苦环绕着我的一生,
像汹涌的大海似的唱着,
而爱的快乐却像鸟儿们在花林里似的唱着。

Love's pain sang round my life like
the unplumbed sea, and love's joy sang like
birds in its flowering groves.

288

假如您愿意,您就熄了灯吧。
我将明白您的黑暗,而且将喜爱它。

Put out the lamp when thou wishest.
I shall know thy darkness and shall love it.

289

当我在那日子的终了,站在您的面前时,
您将看见我的伤疤,而知道我有我的许多创伤,
但也有我的医治的法儿。

When I stand before thee at the day's end
thou shalt see my scars and know that
I had my wounds and also my healing.

290

总有一天,我要在别的世界的晨光里对你唱道:
"我以前在地球的光里,在人的爱里,已经见过你了。"

Some day I shall sing to thee in the sunrise of some other world,
"I have seen thee before in the
light of the earth, in the love of man."

291

从别的日子里飘浮到我的生命里的云，
不再落下雨点或引起风暴了，
却只给予我的夕阳的天空以色彩。

Clouds come floating into my life from other days no longer to shed rain or usher storm but to give colour to my sunset sky.

292

真理引起了反对它自己的狂风骤雨，
那场风雨吹散了真理的广播的种子。

Truth raises against itself the storm that scatters its seeds broadcast.

293

昨夜的风雨给今日的早晨戴上了金色的和平。

The storm of the last night has crowned this morning with golden peace.

294

真理仿佛带了它的结论而来；
而那结论却产生了它的第二个。

Truth seems to come with its final word;
and the final word gives birth to its next.

295

他是有福的,
因为他的名望并没有比他的真实更光亮。

Blessed is he whose fame does
not outshine his truth.

296

您的名字的甜蜜充溢着我的心,
而我忘掉了我自己的——就像您早晨的太阳升起时,
那大雾便消失了。

Sweetness of thy name fills my heart when
I forget mine — like thy morning sun
when the mist is melted.

297

静悄悄的黑夜具有母亲的美丽,
而吵闹的白天具有孩子的美。

The silent night has the beauty of the mother
and the clamorous day of the child.

298

当人微笑时,世界爱了他。
当他大笑时,世界便怕他了。

The world loved man when he smiled.
The world became afraid of him when he laughed.

299

神等待着人在智慧中重新获得童年。

God waits for man to regain his childhood in wisdom.

300

让我感到这个世界乃是您的爱的成形吧,
那么,我的爱也将帮助着它。

Let me feel this world as thy love taking form,
then my love will help it.

301

您的阳光对着我的心头的冬天微笑着,
从来不怀疑它的春天的花朵。

Thy sunshine smiles upon the winter days of my heart,
never doubting of its spring flowers.

302

神在他的爱里吻着"有涯",
而人却吻着"无涯"。

God kisses the finite in his love and
man the infinite.

303

您越过不毛之年的沙漠而到达了圆满的时刻。

Thou crossest desert lands of barren years to reach the moment of fulfilment.

304

神的静默使人的思想成熟而为语言。

God's silence ripens man's thoughts into speech.

305

"永恒的旅客"呀,

你可以在我的歌中找到你的足迹。

Thou wilt find, Eternal Traveller,

marks of thy footsteps across my songs.

306

让我不致羞辱您吧,父亲,

您在您的孩子们身上显现出您的光荣。

Let me not shame thee, Father,

who displayest thy glory in thy children.

307

这一天是不快活的。光在蹙额的云下,
如一个被责打的儿童,灰白的脸上留着泪痕,
风又叫号着,似一个受伤的世界的哭声。
但是我知道,我正跋涉着去会我的朋友。

Cheerless is the day, the light under frowning
clouds is like a punished child with traces of tears
on its pale cheeks, and the cry of
the wind is like the cry of a wounded world.
But I know I am traveling to meet my friend.

308

今天晚上棕榈叶在嚓嚓地作响,

海上有大浪,满月啊,就像世界在心脉悸跳。

从什么不可知的天空,

您在您的沉默里带来了爱的痛苦的秘密?

Tonight there is a stir among the palm leaves, a swell in the sea, Full Moon, like the heart throb of the world. From what unknown sky hast thou carried in thy silence the aching secret of love?

309

我梦见一颗星,一个光明岛屿,我将在那里出生。
在它快速的闲暇深处,
我的生命将成熟它的事业,
像秋天阳光下的稻田。

I dream of a star, an island of light,
where I shall be born and in the depth
of its quickening leisure my life will ripen
its works like the rice-field in the autumn sun.

310

雨中的湿土的气息,

就像从渺小的无声的群众那里来的一阵巨大的赞美歌声。

The smell of the wet earth in the rain rises like

a great chant of praise from the voiceless

multitude of the insignificant.

311

说爱情会失去的那句话,

乃是我们不能够当作真理来接受的一个事实。

That love can ever lose is a fact

that we cannot accept as truth.

312

我们将有一天会明白,
死永远不能够夺去我们的灵魂所获得的东西,
因为她所获得的,和她自己是一体。

We shall know some day that death can never rob us of that which our soul has gained, for her gains are one with herself.

313

神在我黄昏的微光中,带着花到我这里来。
这些花都是我过去之时的,
在他的花篮中还保存得很新鲜。

God comes to me in the dusk of my evening with the flowers from my past kept fresh in his basket.

314

主呀,当我的生之琴弦都已调得谐和时,
你的手的一弹一奏,都可以发出爱的乐声来。

When all the strings of my life will be tuned, my Master, then at every touch of thine
will come out the music of love.

315

让我真真实实地活着吧,我的上帝。
这样,死对于我也就成了真实的了。

Let me live truly, my Lord, so that death to me become true.

316

人类的历史在很忍耐地等待着被侮辱者的胜利。

Man's history is waiting in patience for the triumph of the insulted man.

317

我这一刻感到你的眼光正落在我的心上,
像那早晨阳光中的沉默落在已收获的孤寂的田野上一样。

I feel thy gaze upon my heart this moment
like the sunny silence of the morning upon
the lonely field whose harvest is over.

318

在这喧哗的波涛起伏的海中,
我渴望着咏歌之鸟。

I long for the Island of Songs across this heaving
Sea of Shouts.

319

夜的序曲是开始于夕阳西下的音乐,

开始于它对难以形容的黑暗所作的庄严的赞歌。

The prelude of the night is commenced in the music
of the sunset, in its solemn hymn
to the ineffable dark.

320

我攀登上高峰,

发现在名誉的荒芜不毛的高处,

简直找不到遮身之地。

我的引导者啊,领导着我在光明逝去之前,

进到沉静的山谷里去吧,在那里,

一生的收获将会成熟为黄金的智慧。

I have scaled the peak and found no

shelter in fame's bleak and barren height.

Lead me, my Guide, before the light fades,

into the valley of quiet

where life's harvest mellows

into golden wisdom.

321

在这个黄昏的朦胧里,

好些东西看来都仿佛是幻象一般

——尖塔的底层在黑暗里消失了,

树顶像是墨水的模糊的斑点似的。

我将等待着黎明,而当我醒来的时候,

就会看到在光明里的您的城市。

Things look phantastic in this dimness of the dusk

—the spires whose bases are lost in the dark

and tree tops like blots of ink.

I shall wait for the morning and wake up to see

thy city in the light.

322

我曾经受苦过,曾经失望过,曾经体会过"死亡",
于是我以我在这伟大的世界里为乐。

I have suffered and despaired and known death and I am glad that I am in this great world.

323

在我的一生里,也有贫乏和沉默的地域。
它们是我忙碌的日子得到日光与空气的几片空旷之地。

There are tracts in my life that are bare and silent.

They are the open spaces

where my busy days had their light and air.

324

我的未完成的过去,
从后边缠绕到我身上,使我难于死去。
请从它那里释放了我吧。

Release me from my unfulfilled past clinging
to me from behind making death difficult.

325

"我相信你的爱。"
就让这句话做我的最后的话。

Let this be my last word,
that I trust in thy love.

辑二

生如夏花之绚烂
Living like summer flowers

生如夏花之绚烂

葱茏岁月，往事流转，在被苦难拗成一片荒芜的废园中，有一朵夏花灼灼盛放。不嫣红、不姹紫，却以芬芳惊艳了时光。这朵花，是泰戈尔。

罗宾德拉纳特·泰戈尔，一个用其 80 年的生命将夏花之绚烂与秋叶之静美贯彻凿凿的男人。

泰戈尔出生于印度西孟加拉邦的加尔各答，家境优渥。其父兄皆为社会名流，有着地位最高的婆罗门种姓。他的生活本该一片从容静好，但镌刻在骨血中的倔强、热血和对光明与自由的向往，却促使他在韶华之年选择了出离与叛逆。

14 岁那年，泰戈尔这个家族最小、最受宠溺的男孩，在一家人的瞠目结舌中辍学了。他不愿意回到那让人窒息、刻板且无趣的校园,被传统、迂旧、封建的思想荼毒。为此,身为哲学家的父亲选择了缄默,二兄萨特因既生气又担忧,母亲和姐姐们也都焦急无奈,唯有五兄乔迪满心支持与鼓励。他鼓励弟弟用新的曲调去写诗,介绍他加入以政治解放为目的的社团"生机勃勃会",引导他阅读一些西方的进步书籍,带他参加各种各样的活动……那段时间对泰戈尔来说是格外美好的。然而,所有的美好,多以匆匆为注脚,少有例外。

1878年,刚刚与爱情撞了个满怀,尚且懵懂且青涩的泰戈尔辞别故里,辞别了那个还没等来他告白的姑娘,和兄长萨特因一起远赴英伦。那个时候,他从未想过,此一去,竟是永诀。

在伦敦的日子里,泰戈尔既开怀又郁闷,进步的英伦为他的人生开启了另一道宽广、多彩的门,而无趣且无聊的法律学学习又让他痛苦不堪。于是,这个生性叛逆的男孩再次张扬了他的个性,他自作主张,改学了英国文学和西方音乐。这种做法,让家人极是不满,这种不满,在1880年他孑然一身、无任何学位傍身便回归时被发酵到了极致。

没有人再为他的前途操心,没有人再在他身边唠叨管束,他似乎一下子就自由了。事实上,在这段"自由"的日子里,他也的确随心所欲地创作了不少文学作品,题材包括但不限于诗歌、戏剧、散文、小说。譬如《暮歌》《画与歌》《晨歌》《死亡的贸易》,等等。只不过,不曾被允诺的"自由"终归难以长久。1883年,为了让儿子"收收心",由父亲代为做主,为泰戈尔订了一门亲。

婚姻的到来,让泰戈尔委实有些猝不及防。在一派洋溢的喜气中,他有了一位小他 11 岁、婆罗门家庭出身、朴实、勤劳、贤惠,却没什么文化的"小媳妇",他亲切地叫她莉妮。莉妮为他生了 5 个孩子,她给予他生命中最温暖的 20 年时光;他甘愿欠她一笔情债,允诺要终生偿还以专一的爱。

有了家庭,曾经热血冲动的泰戈尔变得成熟稳重了。1884 年,他加入了社会改革团体——梵社,成为秘书;同时,也接受家族委派,回到家乡,管理祖产和佃户。那段时间,他对底层社会、对祖国、对革命、对国家的发展等都有了更深刻、更清晰的认知,这种认知,从他彼时创作的《刚与柔》《国王与王后》《摩诃摩耶》《缤纷集》《金帆船》《太阳与乌云》《两亩地》等多部作品中都有折射,甚至,为了实现自己在政治、思想上的一些主张,1901 年,他还在圣地尼克坦创办了一所教育实践学校。

然而,平静的背后,酝酿的却是疾风暴雨。1901 年后,命运终于撕去所有的伪装,在泰戈尔面前露出了他狰狞、残忍的一面:相濡以沫的妻子、严肃慈爱的父亲、活泼伶俐的女儿在短短数年的时间里,相继离他而去。巨大的悲痛,令他彷徨无措。

为了麻痹自己,他将全部的精力都投入工作与文学创作中,创作了后来被印度和孟加拉定为国歌的《人民的意志》《金色的孟加拉》

及《戈拉》《顽固堡垒》等一系列反对封建压迫、崇尚自由民主的作品，为当时如火如荼的印度民族解放运动注入了一股思想上的"洪流"，居功甚伟。

然而，在丧妻、丧父、丧女的三重打击之后，命运又和他开了一个恶劣的玩笑。因为理念上的种种分歧，泰戈尔与他服务了十余年之久的梵社最终分道扬镳。

"世界以它的痛苦同我接吻，而要求歌声做报酬。"——他如是说，亦如是做了。

1913年，凭借抒情诗集《吉檀迦利》（中文译名为"献歌"）他出人意料地斩获诺贝尔文学奖，一时名闻遐迩、勋高望重。那时，有人将他与纪伯伦并列，盛赞他们是"站在东西方文化桥梁上的两位巨人"。

人生至此，大概无憾了吧，但如此殊荣对泰戈尔而言，从不是终点，而是起点。获奖后，他的目光并未在咫尺之内的印度停留，而是望向了远方，望向了整个世界。

此后的近30年的岁月里，泰戈尔的足迹踏遍了英国、法国、日本、中国、美国、俄罗斯等诸多国家，在那里，和他的双足一起伫留的，还有他的笔、他的诗、他自由的思想、他博爱的胸怀、他缤纷的文字、他愤怒的呐喊、他振聋发聩的呼唤……

1916年，泰戈尔身履日本，在这个新兴的资本主义国度，他看到了生机勃勃的一面,也看到了落后跋扈的一面,感慨良多;1919年,阿姆利泽惨案震惊世界,曾旅居英国、身具英国爵士爵位的泰戈尔愤怒萦胸,断然放弃了爵士的头衔并发文谴责;1924年,踩着仲夏融融的阳光,已然声誉全球的泰戈尔来到了向往的中国,在清华大学发表了热情洋溢的演讲,字字温暖而发人深省;1930年,他即兴创作了《俄罗斯书简》,对刚刚访问过的、朝气蓬勃的苏联做了深情地赞美与讴歌……及后数年,德意日陆续发动战争,全世界都被"二战"的阴云笼罩,泰戈尔拍案愤起,以大无畏的态度,冒着重重危险,向全世界人民发出"准备战斗吧,反抗那披着人皮的野兽"的呼吁,声声动情。

若能青春复壮年,这位虔诚相信:"苦难能照亮前路,负担会变成礼物"的"斗士"定会昂首迈向战场吧!只可惜,彼时的他,年早耄耋。

岁月剥离了他的所有,他却仍在岁月里孤独地放歌;世界欺骗了他,他却执拗地坚持着。在生命最后的日子里,他仍渴望为这个纷乱的、充满了抗争的世界做些什么:1941年4月,《文明的危机》在血与火中问世。同年8月,这位80岁高龄的"斗士"在加尔各答的祖宅溘然长逝。

泰戈尔走了,而凝结着他所有智慧、情感、思想、感悟的50多部诗集、100多篇小说、30余部剧本和多不可胜计的一首首歌却为他续起了另一段非凡的生命长桥。

对这位享誉世界的文学巨匠,我们终究难以用是与非、粉与黑去简单而直白地评判。但我们应当庆幸,曾有这样一个人,以诗意书写着远方;曾有这样一个人,将"生如夏花之绚烂"的自由与美好带给人间。

/ 愿生如夏花 /

飞 鸟 集

选题策划： 上央图书
文图编辑： 王松慧
美术编辑： 刘晓东
封面设计： 段　瑶
版式设计： 蒋碧君
图片提供： 视觉中国